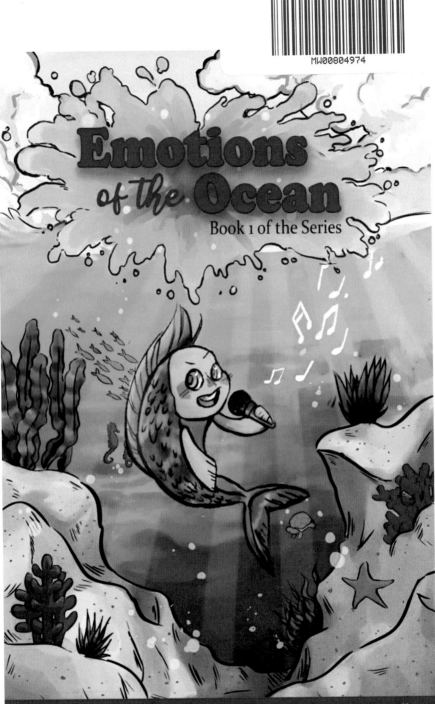

Emotions
of the Ocean

Book 1 of the Series

Written by Tania Isley Robinson and Illustrated by Hope Powell

Emotions of the Ocean

the Ocean

Book One: The Shadow

WRITTEN BY/ILLUSTRATED BY

Tania Isley Robinson
& Hope Powell

Copyright © 2019 by Tania Isley-Robinson
Published by BlackGold Publishing

1706 Todds Lane, Suite 258
Hampton, VA 23666

First Edition: December 20, 2020
Printed in the United States of America
ISBN: 978-1-7345083-7-6

"Dedicated to all of the innocents I know…
those who have always showed me the
importance of using your imagination."

OCEAN TIDES

Ocean Tides is way down in the ocean, I can't tell you how far we are because I really don't know. Not to mention, our normally quiet city was threatened by who we call "The Bubble Makers," better known as Strangers of the Ocean, but we'll get into that later on in my story. By the way, you can call me Mr. Blue, I've lived in Ocean Tides for almost 60 years. As you know, blue whales live a pretty long time.

I've seen a lot in my life but I did not expect to see Ocean Tides change the way it has in the past couple of years.

I don't really say much, I'm not a big talker, you can say I'm an observer but really I'm merely taking everything in.

Ocean Tides has a population of 300 sea creatures; we have a pretty tight knit community. We have many different types of underwater animals, but we all coexist peacefully. Some more creative and unique then others but we'll get into that soon. Mayor Finnster has done a good job of keeping order, a while ago we had a bad shark invasion and a lot of homes were burglarized - it was unsafe but thankfully they were caught and thrown in the net. Mayor Finnster, now that's a good guy and his son Finn has an even bigger heart. Ocean Tides is filled with great friendships, warm families, and shows you that you don't have to be from the same egg patch to be a family. You can often see twins Ed and Erica encouraging each other and giving each other high fives while out playing together, but they care for and encourage their friends as often as they do to each other. It's also filled with elders who understand it's rich history. Elders such as Miss Tutti and Mr. Willie the creative teachers at one of the schools, the Deep Blue School, who would do anything for the unique batch of students that attend their school.

Police detectives, Mr. and Mrs. Jellyfish who, along with Major Finnster help keep our city safe. And the most entertaining of them all, Mrs. Blanche Turtle, known to the children of Ocean Tides as Grandma Turtle. Many think that she is eccentric but she is extremely caring especially in deciding to take over the care of her grandchild Marvin after the death of his parents. I guess you can call me an admirer of Blanche Turtles'. She also is caregiver to most of the children of Ocean Tides while their parents are at work, telling them all kinds of outrageous stories.

Then you have people who are not so nice, like Miss Marli and Mr. Omar, the principal of the Deep Blue School and her personal assistant/secretary who have a selfish interest. Their schemes and sabotage almost destroyed the Deep Blue School and Ocean Tides. Before I get into that part of the story, let me first introduce these 9 unique sea creatures that make up the ***Emotions of the Ocean.***

FYN THE SAD FISH

Fyn is the most sensitive creature of Emotions of the Ocean . I've known him since he was only a baby. He gets his passion from his parents, Mayor and Mrs. Finnster. I remember when Mayor Finnster was first running for office, he and Mrs. Finnster would bring Fyn in as a guppy and he would look at them with such admiration.

Mrs. Finnster has always been supportive of her husband, as well as Fyn's outrageous causes although Mayor Finnster can admit that his son's ideas may be out of his reach. Fyn's causes include, "Let's Regulate the Salt in the Ocean," campaign, "Pen Pal a Shark," and "Let's Clean the Seaweed," just to name a few. As a guppy his parents became aware of just how sensitive he was, so he no longer accompanies his father on city business trips and his mother does not allow him to watch the news because both would always end in tears for Fyn or result in him throwing himself on the ground crying and not moving - a very intense temper tantrum known as "coffin," by his family and friends. Fyn's friends; Marvin the Shy Turtle, Sherman the

Shrimp, and Erica the Dolphin love and support Fyn and all of his causes despite his swift mood changes - though Fyn never really thinks his causes through. Mrs. Finnster thinks they are 'all great ideas' but even still, Fyn can always hear his mom's voice echoing in the back of his head;

"You have great ideas and a big heart, but you can't save the whole ocean." Those words would often haunt Fyn but he would eagerly reply; "Yes, I can. One day..." in a tone as soft as a whisper.

He walks over to mirror with a can of mousse for his mohawk. It's the first day of school and he is very excited. Fyn is a black fish with blue scales, his Mohawk is black and blue and is brushed forward. He has droopy sympathetic eyes and long eyelashes which add to his dramatic look. Fyn's mouth and lips look like they are in a constant state of pouting. His moves are slow, focused and always with passion. Fyn is so excited for the first day of school that he can hardly contain himself. Even Tonya, the mail lady heard all about how he's excited to go to his new school with his friends and to start learning again. Fyn thinks to himself that he can't wait to see his favorite teacher Miss Tutti as he gazes at a picture of the two of them at his kindergarten graduation way before the new Deep Blue School was ever built. He's known her all his life.

Fyn swims downstairs to the kitchen where his father is reading the newspaper. Mrs. Finnster is at the stove preparing pancakes when Fyn comes over and states, "I am having cereal for breakfast. Every box of Fish Flakes I eat, $1 is donated to a guppy in need." Mrs. Finnster smiles and says, "Ok sweetie." Fyn takes two boxes and says, "I'm taking them for lunch." "Fyn," Mr. Finnster says when his son enters the kitchen, "would you like to ride with me to the school? I have to go there today for the grand opening." Fyn says, "No, dad, I'm going to take the bus. You should come too, it would save on energy and it would look good, you know, you riding to the new school." Mr. Finnster makes a face when Fyn looks away, as the thought of riding with 20 little creatures as precocious as his son pops into his head. Mr. Finnster pushed for this school to be opened especially for children like his son and his friends. He is hoping that this adjustment will be a smooth one for the city. Mrs. Finnster glares are her husband, "That

IS a good idea honey." And he says, "I have a lot to do today, so maybe next time. Have a great day at school though Fyn." Fyn nods and rushes down Aqua Block to the bus stop to see his best friends Sherman and Marvin.

As he approaches, he hears Sherman talking excitedly about how his brothers went to the Navy and he finally has the house and his parents to himself. Marvin's shell is shaking ever so slightly and his head is half way in as he listens to Sherman's rant. Marvin comes out of his shell says, "Hey, Fyn!" and quickly puts his head back in. Sherman states, "Hey there Finnster!" and the three friends wait together for the bus. The baby blue bus approaches with the letters DEEP BLUE SCHOOL and the driver Maggie the Seal greets the children. "Hey there guys! Come on in!"

Fyn and Sherman get on the bus and Marvin is hesitant and shakes a bit before he gets on the bus as well. Maggie states, "What's wrong with him?" Fyn turns back to the entrance of the bus toward Marvin.

Marvin is shaking miserably, scared and apprehensive to get onto the bus. "It's okay Marvin, we're doing this together." Fyn reassures, stepping back outside to offer him a hand. Marvin wearily takes it and enters the bus with him. Marvin gets into the front seat slowly next to Sherman, refuses to make eye contact with anyone else and puts his head back into his shell and says "Let me know when we are  there."

Marvin is very nervous on the first day; Sherman is calm whereas Fyn greets everyone that comes on the bus. Fyn is sitting close the driver as they drive through Ocean Tides. "Don't forget to stop there. We need to get her. Don't forget him." is what Sherman and Marvin overhear Fyn stating to a bus driver as they talk. "Fyn," Sherman says when Marvin gets quiet, "I'm sure the driver knows what she's doing." Fyn states, "I'm just making sure. I don't want anyone to miss the first day of school." Sherman states quietly to Marvin that Fyn is being obsessive about school as it were on of his causes. Sherman is relieved that Henry the bull Shark is no longer allowed to take the bus since all the children petitioned to remove him from taking the bus.

Mr. Finnster looks out of the window to see his son and two friends get on the bus, he states, "They did a good job on the bus. It almost looks like the regular public school bus." Mrs. Finnster gathers up his lunch and walks him to the front door as a moving truck turns onto Aqua Block. "Try not to worry dear, have a good day." Mr. Finnster pecks her on the cheek and says, "You too honey."

As the school bus drives through Ocean Tides Fyn looks out on his hometown. The businesses are very bright and colorful, the bus passes the Ocean Tides Market, the Swim & Shop and the Ocean Tides Police Department. They continue to drive up the hill to an even brighter section of the ocean where the water is totally crystal clear. All the kids look out the window as they approach Ocean Drive. Marvin even pokes his head out of his shell to look. Ocean Drive is comprised of very large and colorful houses which are all different shapes. It is where all of the affluent residents of Ocean Tides live except for Mr. Finnster who wanted buy a home in him and his wife's old neighborhood. Sherman turns to Fyn teasingly and states, "Fyn, you could've lived here so you could be close to your girlfriend Erica." He and Marvin giggle as Fyn rolls his eyes as they approach Ocean Drive Estates where the dolphins live.

Erica sees the bus and runs out before the light turns green to see Fyn. The driver opens the door for Erica to approach and she states, "Hey Fyn. Good luck on your first day. I have to go see Miss Annette at the Ocean Tides Public School but I will over there later." Fyn looks a bit sad but says, "Ok." Sherman and Marvin are giggling as Erica says to them, "Hey Marvin. Hey Shrimpie." Marvin pokes his head back into his shell, shaking it ever so slightly to acknowledge that he saw Erica as Sherman turns red and shakes his fist at her.

Erica's brother, Ed comes out of their house still in his pajamas eating a slice of pizza for breakfast. Erica says, "Ed, are you going on the bus? What are you doing?" Ed stares at the kids and the bus stating, "I'm not taking the bus, I'm going to have the driver take me." Erica rolls her eyes, turns back and says, "Hey Fyn," showing him the box of Fish Flakes in her book bag as he smiles at her. As the bus continues to the school, they pass Ocean Tides Memorial Hospital where Mr.

and Mrs. Dolphin, Ed and Erica's parents, are well-respected surgeons.

The children look out the window and see photographers standing in front of the house of Edgardo Santiago, famous retired baseball player. In front of his home, Mr. Santiago has a large statue of himself in the baseball uniform and holding the bat that he was using when he won the Ocean Series 10 years ago. Edgardo Junior, better known as Eggy is seen getting into his mother's car. When the bus stops next to his house, Eggy looks over at the bus, adjusts his clothing and winks.

The children all look at him in awe and wave excitedly as the girls all scream in enthusiasm, thinking that Eggy is winking at *them* personally. No one is actually aware that Eggy was simply looking at his own reflection in the bus. Eggy was extremely good looking, had strong build for his edge, endless connections thanks to father and everyone in Ocean Tides either wanted to be him or *be with him.* "I can't believe that idiot is going to our school." Sherman states enviously as the bus slowly drives away from the Santiago residence, leaving the children fawning at his departure.

The bus drives down the hill where the ocean gets a little darker and you can see the seaweed coming through a little more. Over in a corner, there is a large sign announcing they had arrived at "DEEP BLUE SCHOOL." Fyn sees his father at the entrance of the school talking to reporters. The bus driver opens the door and says to the children, "Have a good day kids!"

Fyn excitedly yells; "WE'RE HERE!"

Miss Tutti is happily arranging her classroom. She is very excited to start the new school year in a new school. She will miss working side by side with her best friend Annette at the public school but the pilot program at this new school was too good an opportunity to miss. Miss Tutti was specially selected by Mayor Finnster due to her passion and love for helping children, especially those with special needs. Miss Tutti is a seahorse with short curly hair. She is very soft spoken and has a bright, warm and welcoming smile which makes it easy for the children to respond to her. Miss Tutti is also very visual and has a fun and creative teaching style that the children love. She reads the list of her students that she will have this year, while she sets up the seating arrangements. "Fyn, I have sit him in the front because he's so excited about learning. Marvin, I'm going to sit behind Fyn because he doesn't like to be in the front and he always sits behind Fyn. Sherman, Henry, oh wow, Henry the bull shark... I have to put him on the other side so I can watch him. 'Jane and Ovaltine,' she reads her paperwork, 'they will start tomorrow.' She continues to read, "Eggy, Divine, Tamria, Ed."

"How's it going in here?" Mr. Willie, the music teacher says as he pops his head into his wife's classroom. "It's good, I have a very good mix of children this year." Mr. Willie gazes at her list curiously, "Who are they?'" He points to Ovaltine and Jane's names which he does not recognize. "They are the jellyfish family that just moved into town, the parents are the newest Detectives with the Ocean Tides Police Department" Miss Tutti says. "This should be interesting with Henry in the same classroom with the children of police officers." Miss Tutti shakes her head at him, *"It will be fine."*

"Have you seen Miss Marli yet?" Miss Tutti asks. Mr. Willie turns around and makes a sour face and says, "That fathead is floating around somewhere in the hallway. Better yet, I better scram!"

"OOOOOMMMMMMMAAAAAAARRRRRRRRR!" Miss Marli barks as she straightens up her office. Omar slides in quickly. " Y-yes, Miss Marli?" He timidly replies. "WHERE IS MY CUP OF COFFEE OMAR?! I'm getting upset!"

Miss Marli is a blob fish. The blob fish is known to be the ugliest animal in the ocean. Her body is gray and jelly like with no muscles so she floats around without really moving.

Miss Marli also despised children but got a very healthy pay raise from teaching at the public school to become a principal at the Deep Blue School. Miss Marli beat out Miss Tutti for the position of principal after Omar cheated by stealing Miss Tutti's votes. Omar turns quickly, "Of c-course Miss Marli, here you are…" promptly handing Miss Marli her coffee. "This school is probably not going to stay open that long, you know these kids are a bunch of failures. We can go back to the public school and you will soon become principal there." Miss Marli stretches her face into an ugly smile… "Yes… all in due time." There are noises in the hallway and Miss Marli asks Omar to close her office door, "Those little things are here." As a pair, Marli the blob fish and Omar the eel is a slippery and deceitful duo – even if Omar is merely just scared of her overall.

After concluding his first day back at school for the year, the bus drops Fyn back off in front of his house as he notices a moving truck across the street. He sees his father and mother speaking to two jellyfish. Fyn barely hears anything as his eyes lock on the most beautiful creature he has ever seen. He finds himself in a daze as he stares with his mouth open and eyes open wide, as he hears the seashells playing soft romantic music in the background.

Fyn gulped. *"Whoooo is that…?"*

THE JELLYFISH FAMILY

The Jellyfish family's daughter Jane was breathtakingly beautiful. Her jelly like skin sparkles in a light pinkish purple tone and she has bright green eyes and long lashes. Her hair flows and she has long bangs almost matching her lovely eyelashes. Jane is long all the way down to her tentacles. Fyn is amazed by all of her beauty.

Jane is looking at her reflection as she holds a hand mirror, admiring her hair. Fyn can't see anything but Jane as his father is attempting an introduction with the new neighbors.

"This is my son Fyn. Fyn this is Mr. and Mrs. Jellyfish, they just moved in and will be working at the police department. That is their daughter Jane and you have a son?" Suddenly there is a distracting crash and out of the moving truck there is a large ball with tentacles flying everywhere that rolls into Jane who then drops and breaks her mirror. Fyn suddenly breaks out of his trance. Mrs. Jellyfish replies, "and our son Ovaltine." Jane looks over at Ovaltine annoyed. "Ugh, I don't know why we had to bring him with us!" She storms back into the house. Ovaltine quickly stands up excitedly, "Hey, Mr. Mayor, hey Mrs. Mayor, hey little guy. I am Ovaltine but you can call me Busy Octo, all my friends call me Busy Octo."

Busy Octo is a large octopus who is a bright orange and yellow color. Fyn was taken off guard as he stares at Busy Octo whose hat was spinning. Busy Octo continues to talk rapidly. Mrs. Jellyfish interrupts him, "Ovaltine, can you please go straighten up your room? Just concentrate on your room, ok? Nothing else." Mrs. Jellyfish says as Busy takes a free tentacle and shakes Fyn's fin.

"My name is Fyn; Fyn is my name. I'm Fyn." As Fyn tries to let go of Busy Octo's tentacle. Mrs. Jellyfish gently breaks the hold that Ovaltine has on Fyn's fin and he hurries away. "Ok, I guess I'll see you guys later!" Mrs. Jellyfish says. "If she didn't interrupt him, Ovaltine would be out here for days talking." Mr. Jellyfish says, "We adopted Ovaltine a couple of months ago. He's a bit hyperactive." Mr. Finnster responds, "…Well, that's okay. He must be adjusting to the change of scenery." Mr. and Mrs. Jellyfish look at each other and smile, as if they know something their new neighbors don't. Mrs. Finnster catches their glance and clears his throat, "What I mean is… He sure does have a lot of character." Fyn coughs and says under his breath, "A little *too* much."

After the introduction, Fyn enters his room and lays on the bed as he thinks about Jane. He wonders if she will be going to his school or the public school. Fyn is already sure that Busy Octo will be.

Jane walks through the bathroom into Ovaltine's room. He is unpacking his boxes but making a bigger mess - he starts to unpack contents from one box then goes to another, never finishing unpacking any boxes. Eventually he just empties boxes onto his bed, he has several items in his tentacles and when Jane enters his room and he drops everything on the floor. "What are you doing Busy Octo?" Ovaltine is super disorganized, his room is chaotic and he is all over the place. He looks at her confused. "I'm unpacking, mom said I need to straighten up my room." Jane looks at him with an attitude. "I don't know why you're doing all this. You know mom is just going to come in and straighten it up for you anyway, like she always does." She turns and leaves the room and Ovaltine continues to try to straighten up the growing mess in his room. Suddenly, Jane hears her mom's voice in Ovaltine's room helping him straighten up. Aggravated, she closes the door that separates her room from the bathroom she and Ovaltine share. As she is unpacking, she comes across her collection of "Ocean Beautiful" magazine. She lives by these magazines and reads them every night before she goes to bed. Jane pushes a box labeled 'beauty items' into the bathroom and she sees that Busy Octo has dumped his own items into the bathroom sink. As she stares at the sink with all Busy Octo's stuff in it, unable to see the bottom she looks in the mirror and notices her skin getting red from its normal light pink-purple color and her tentacles start to spark. Suddenly, around her she feels everything start to shake, Jane grabs the sink as the mirror over the sink starts to wobble and cracks.

A small octopus sits on a bench at the Seaweed Police Department. His eyes are puffy as if he's been crying, his tentacles don't even reach the floor, one tentacle is holding a blanket, the other a book bag. He looks around the police station, in hopes that he will see his parents who have finally come to pick him up. 30 minutes turn into an hour, then two. A uniformed jellyfish comes to the young octopus with a lady from the OPS (Ocean Protective Services).

Mrs. Jellyfish approaches, "Hey Ovaltine, that's your name right?" Ovaltine shakes his head up and down. Mrs. Jellyfish continues, "This is Ms. Garrison from OPS, you're going to go with her." As Ms. Garrison approaches, Ovaltine clumsily knocks over some things on a nearby desk and mumbles 'No" and starts backing away from her and Mrs. Jellyfish. With his tentacles he continues to knock things over as he heads for the door. He goes into the nearest corner and collapses, curls up and begins to cry. Mrs. Jellyfish goes over to console him, while she is embracing him, they lock eyes and her hear melts. "Don't worry Ovaltine, *I'm going to take care of you.*

Mrs. Jellyfish files away Ovaltine's adoption papers. She will never forget the day that she saw that poor little octopus looking scared and alone in the police station. She did not know how things would eventually turn out, but what she knew was that she could not leave him without a mother. Mr. Jellyfish comes into the office with more boxes. "This is going to be a good fresh start for all of us." Mrs. Jellyfish smiles, "Yes, the Finnsters seem really nice. I think Jane and Ovaltine will do well here. I think they will make a lot of friends at the Deep Blue School and I'm happy that they will finally be in school together."

MARVIN THE SHY TURTLE

Marvin gets off the bus down the block from his house. He walks slowly up the block with his head still peeking out of his shell, all you can see is the brim of his hat. Sheila the clam, Marvin's friend calls out to him. "Hey Marvin!" Startled, Marvin sticks his entire head into his shaking shell and looks around. Sheila hops to his side.

"It's just me."

As all you can see is curls coming out of her clam. Marvin pokes his head out a bit and says, "Oh hey." They walk alongside each other. Sheila asks him, "How was your first day at Deep Blue?" Marvin responds, "It was ok, how about you?" Sheila answers, "It was okay too but I miss having classes with you guys." After Sheila and Marvin say goodbye, Marvin walks up to his house and notices yet another box at the front door and he can hear the TV from outside. Marvin steps into the front door bringing the box with him. "Grandma! Grandma, turn your TV down, you can hear it from outside!" Marvin says as he walks into the house. He walks into the room where his grandmother is seated – eating a snack, on the phone and watching the

Ocean Shopping Channel placing an order. "Grandma, what are you doing?" Grandma in her southern accent responds, "I'm ordering cream Marvin, from the TV... Now you say I get a free gym membership for a month?" Grandma Turtle asks the representative on the phone. Marvin is looking at the TV in disbelief. "Grandma, the cream is $500! ...And what do you mean the gym? And you can't go to the gym, you walk with a cane. YOU HAVE A CANE!" Grandma Turtle ignores Marvin's obvious comment and yells over the TV, "Marvin, take the box into the room with the others." Marvin, seeing that this conversation is pointless, turns and takes the box into the cluttered guest where about 50 other boxes sit unopened.

Grandma Turtle is Marvin's maternal grandmother. She is in her 60s but she appears younger, despite her bad knees. She is very fashionable, having her hair and nails always done. Grandma Turtle has been a constant figure in Marvin's life since he hatched. She took primary care of him since his parents' passing. Marvin comes back to Grandma Turtle who is now off the phone.

"Hey Marvin, how was your first day of school? Can you grab me a glass a water?"

Marvin doesn't answer because he is so overwhelmed by all of the toys all over the living room they were left by the children his grandmother cares for during the day. As Grandma Turtle goes into the pocket of her housecoat, she takes out several different color pills which are mixed with change, tissues, chocolates and candies.

Marvin heads into the kitchen to get his grandma's water and notices she's left the stove on again. He rushes back to her side.

"GRANDMA! Did you know that the stove was on!?" Grandma takes the glass out of Marvin's hand, ignoring his question and asks, "Well, is the stew bubbling yet?" He looks at her and shakes his head, "…Grandma, you could've burned down the house." Marvin gets a sudden mental image of his house burning while his grandmother is on the phone placing an order and he cannot get in to help her because all of the boxes are everywhere, in front of the door. His thoughts are interrupted by his grandmother standing in front of him. "Marvin, you know what I saw today on the television? I saw this program about a one eyed fish who follows children home who walk on the cracks of the sidewalk and takes them. Do you walk on the cracks?" Marvin puts his whole head in his shell and starts to shake, overwhelmed. "Marvin, don't worry, get outta there. You're ok, you don't walk on the cracks like I told you." Grandma Turtle laughs and takes her cane as she walks away.

Grandma Turtle continues as she walks back into the living room. "You 'member what I told you, walk on the cracks, get attacked!" Marvin stays in place, nervous and shaking in his shell as his usually does from his grandmother's rants.

Marvin finally exits after Grandma Turtle focuses back on the TV long enough to stop talking, and goes to his room, takes his hat off and puts it in his special box. He stares at it for a moment before putting it into the box. The hat was given to him by his parents before they passed. Since he was quite young, it is the only gift that he has from them. He slowly puts his hat into the box, then puts that box into a larger one which he then puts under his bed. Marvin takes several books and magazines out of his shell and puts them on his bookshelf. Marvin likes to read and he has tons' books and magazines pertaining to Biology, Marine Biology, History, Astrology. He likes to get lost in these books because he feels that he can't really get away from his regular life and he feels safe in his head because he can control that world, which is his imagination. Marvin takes out a book which has a bunch of stars on it and sits quietly in the corner of his room and begins to read it.

5, 4, 3, 2, 1... blast off!

Marvin gets lost in the book about space and imagines himself as an astronaut who is about to orbit into space. He sees himself on the space shuttle in full astronaut uniform on the rocket which is now shaking as it is begins to take off into outer space. Marvin starts to shake as well as his room. Marvin looks up from the book to see that his room is still shaking, his books all start to fall off of the shelves and tumble onto him. He nervously pokes his head back inside his shell.

SHERMAN THE SHRIMP

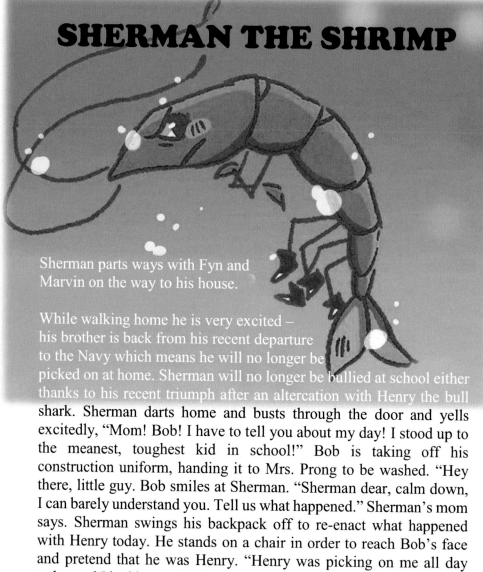

Sherman parts ways with Fyn and Marvin on the way to his house.

While walking home he is very excited – his brother is back from his recent departure to the Navy which means he will no longer be picked on at home. Sherman will no longer be bullied at school either thanks to his recent triumph after an altercation with Henry the bull shark. Sherman darts home and busts through the door and yells excitedly, "Mom! Bob! I have to tell you about my day! I stood up to the meanest, toughest kid in school!" Bob is taking off his construction uniform, handing it to Mrs. Prong to be washed. "Hey there, little guy. Bob smiles at Sherman. "Sherman dear, calm down, I can barely understand you. Tell us what happened." Sherman's mom says. Sherman swings his backpack off to re-enact what happened with Henry today. He stands on a chair in order to reach Bob's face and pretend that he was Henry. "Henry was picking on me all day today and I had it mom! After class in the hallway, he pushed me into my locker and that was it. I turned around and before I knew what I was doing, I pushed him! Then I darted up into his face and told him about himself. Everything went quiet and all I could see was the space between his eyes, that's how close I was…" Sherman pauses to catch his breath. Mrs. Prong looks surprised at her young son. "Oh my…" she mutters. Sherman continues, "I told him that I was tired of him picking on me and how he's just a bully and he has nothing better to do. I told him that he's going to end up like his father in the net." Mrs. Prong looks a bit disappointed in her son. "I'm glad you stood up for yourself Sherman, but that comment about his father was not nice." Bob interjects to get back to the story. "And what happened after?" He asks enthusiastically. Sherman turns from his mom's disappointment and to Bob and continues "…I told him that he's just a big head and taking up space at the school! And that this was the last day he would ever pick on me! I darted off and turned around to see if he was following me… but he wasn't! Can you believe it?!" Bob pats Sherman, "I'm proud of you little guy." Sherman smiles and turns back to his mom. "Mom, I want a snack." Mrs. Prong looks sideways at her son, "You mean please make you a snack?" Sherman puts his head down slightly, "Yes, sorry mom." Bob starts for the front door, "Hey little guy, can you help me get some stuff in from the truck?"

Sherman, feeling so powerful and bigger than his small size puts Bob's construction hat on confidently and heads for the door following his stepfather out. Bob tells Sherman to put the pieces of wood in the garage and begins to give instructions on how he should line it up. Sherman dismisses him, insisting he knows what he is doing. "I got it. I got it." After Bob leaves the garage, Sherman begins talking to himself. "…*No one is gonna mess with me now.*" Sherman stacks the wood in the garage as he does fighting moves and karate chops in the air. He throws his punches in the direction of the wood, pretending to break a few pieces.

Kick, punch, chop!

Suddenly, the whole garage begins to shake and several pieces of wood that he has stacked begins to fall. Bob appears at the garage door and grabs Sherman out of the harm's way, holding him against his body and he carries

Sherman as everything around them begins to shake.

HENRY THE BULL SHARK

Henry puts on his spiked helmet and gets on his bike, simultaneously knocking over the other bikes on the rack in front of the school. As he is riding, the fish bones in his spokes rattle. Everyone gets out of his way as he rides off of school grounds. As Henry is riding, a smirk forms on his face as he recalls the altercation he had with Sherman.

In his mind he replays Sherman's words, "You're just a big bully! You're gonna be just like your father." As Sherman's words sink in, Henry pedals faster and gets angry. He begins to remember how his mom cried at the courthouse when his dad, uncles and the bull shark gang was sentenced to The Net. He recalls his mom crying on the phone, talking to his dad about money and since the government seized his bank accounts, Mrs. Bullshark had to start over. Henry rides faster stating;

"...I'm *nothing* like my father..."

As he gets closer to his house, he jumps off of his bike and let's it run into the mailbox at the front of his apartment complex. He picks up his bike and carries it into the building. Henry laughs to himself, thinking back to Sherman and says aloud "...that little guy has heart." He wishes he could go off like that on his father for how he left him and his mom.

Henry texts his mom "home" but then quickly recalls how she likes to hear his voice so he calls her at work. "Hello, can I speak to Nurse Rebecca?" After about 3 minutes, Henry hears his mom's voice. "Henry? Honey are you home? How was school?" Henry answers, "School was school." His mom continues… "Did you get into any trouble today?" Henry thinks to himself before answering what his mom wants to hear, "Not really." His mom pauses for a second, unsure is she should believe him, "Henry…." She begins but then hears over the PA system, "Nurse Rebecca to ICU." Henry is aggravated that his mom has to work so much now. "Ok, bye mom." Henry's mom tries to remember everything before getting off the phone with her son. "Ok, stay in today and make sure you lock the doors. There is a list on the counter of things I need you to do. Be a good boy. I love you and I'll see you later on tonight." Henry realizes how much he misses having his mom home when he got out of school before she had to pick up an extra shift. "Ok mom, love you too." Henry hangs up the phone and goes over to the list.

Henry takes chicken nuggets out of the freezer and throws them in the sink to defrost them for dinner. He reaches for a container of ice cream that is in the freezer before he sees his mom's post-it, it reads "NO HENRY HONEY, THAT'S NOT A SNACK XOXO." Henry puts the ice cream back and grabs a banana and apple out of the fruit basket to eat. He goes to his room which is a mess, instead of cleaning his room as the list says, Henry throws his backpack into the room and heads back into the living room, puts his feet up and watches TV. He hears people yelling in the hallway and turns the TV up. His eyes wander to the family picture that hangs above the TV of him, his mother and father. Henry stares at the picture as a

tear forms in his eye. The frame starts to shake, falls down and breaks. Henry holds onto the chair, unable to get up as everything begins to fall to the ground around him.

ED AND ERICA DOLPHIN

Mr. and Mrs. Dolphin are talking while walking up the steps of Ocean Tides Public School. "I wonder what it's going to look like on Ed's transcript that he goes to a special school?" Mr. Dolphin says to his wife. Mrs. Dolphin replies "I wonder how much worse it would look that he's a trouble maker at the regular school."

Ed is leaning on the wall listening to his music with his eyes closed. Ed hears footsteps as he walks as he lowers the music and opens his eyes as he sees his parents coming up the steps. His father is wearing an expensive gray suit with a stethoscope around his neck. He always has that around his neck everywhere he goes. He knows it annoys his mom, because he also wears it when we go out to dinner. Ed asked him once, "Why do you always wear that on your neck outside of the hospital?" His father answered, "I want everyone to know there's a doctor in the building because you never know when there will be an emergency son." *I think that's crap. I just think he likes to show off and impress people…* Ed thought to himself. Everyone knows who he is, he tries to always be on television with his old childhood friend, Mr. Finnster. Especially taking on controversial medical procedures. Ed thinks to himself, *Dad must be mad she's wearing a pantsuit, I bet he tried to get her to wear a dress this morning. She obviously won that argument like she does most of the time. That's the go to.*

Ed goes over to his mom and gives her a hug.

"They're kicking me out Mom?" Ed gives her his best sad face. Mrs. Dolphin tries to keep a positive face. "No honey, they're just suggesting that you go to another school where you can excel." Mr. Dolphin responds, "They're kicking you out." The Dolphins family walks into the school. As they walk in the hallway, teachers fix themselves up and pop their heads out to get a look at Ed's famous parents. Mr. Dolphin shakes a couple of teachers and student's hands. Even teachers and students that didn't have their hands out. Ed and Mrs. Dolphin laugh at Mr. Dolphin's expense as they walk into the guidance counselor's office. Erica is already in the guidance counselor's office when her parents and brother arrive. "I just want to say thank you for this opportunity and I can assure you I will take this very seriously." The guidance counselor smiles "Erica you really deserve it, both the principal and vice principal signed off on this already. You have been a great asset to this school and your assistance is greatly appreciated. You can just sign here, and your parents will sign here." Ed sits in a chair and turns his music back on and his sister turns around and sticks out her tongue at him. Ed makes rings around his eyes to make fun of his sister's glasses. "How will Erica's time be split between here and the other school?" Mr. Dolphin asks concerned. "We have spoken to Erica's teachers and she has excelled in her classes so we are sure this will be fine. We are going to be very flexible." The guidance counselor replied. "I can do this. I have very good time management skills." Erica replies hopefully looking at her mom. Mr. Dolphin looks convinced "If she says she can do it, let her do it." Ed perks up, "She just wants to be closer to her over dramatic boyfriend so they can cry and save the world together." Mr. Dolphin laughs, and his wife looks frustrated. "Ed, *that is not nice.*" The Dolphins sign Erica's paper. "The car service is waiting for you both to take you to the school. Erica looks confused, "So you guys aren't coming with us to the Deep Blue School?" Mr. Dolphins shakes his head. "Your mom and I have an important appointment in a ½ hour so we're hoping this won't take long." Erica steps towards the door. "So, I'm going to talk to some of my teachers and I'll be in the car."

"As you know, the counselor begins, "after talking to Ed's teachers and the rest of the administration, it was recommended, actually highly recommended that your son goes to a school which can better serve his behavioral needs. Though Ed gets straight A's after his finishes his work, he gets disruptive." Mr. Dolphin begins to get angry. "It's probably because he's bored. Maybe the teachers need to give out harder work?" Mrs. Dolphin tries to defuse the situation. "Maybe they could give him more work." Ed interrupts quickly. "I'm not doing any extra work!" The guidance counselor puts up a piece of paper. "This is the paper that all of Ed's teachers signed withdrawing him from all of his classes effective tomorrow. We just need your signatures and he can begin the Deep Blue School tomorrow." Ed senses his parents' disappointment as he hands them the paper after signing. "It's cool. Edgardo Santiago is at that school. I'm gonna make him my best friend. You know his
dad is a famous baseball player." Mr. Dolphin looks annoyed. "And YOUR dad is a famous surgeon."

Erica hangs up the phone with Miss Tutti after confirming the beginning of her internship tomorrow and stating that she is going to the Deep Blue School to fill out paperwork. Erica sees Ed dragging his feet as he walks to the car. She is immediately annoyed at the sight of her lazy brother. "Why do you always have to shed the light on this family in a negative way?" Erica says angrily. "Attention is attention. I don't think this family cares what kind.

You're just mad because no attention is on you and your stupid internship." Erica tries to act unfazed. "You're an idiot." Ed and Erica bicker back and forth throughout the remainder of the car ride.

Suddenly the car begins to shake uncontrollably.

They attempt to put their seat belts on but the car is shaking too much. Ed and Erica hug each other while the car and ground continues to shake.

EGGY THE PUFF FISH

Edgardo is standing outside of the school as his mom rolls up in her fancy sports car. Mrs. Santiago exits the car and rushes to hug her son. She is dressed in her typical animal print and tights pants; she yells to her son with her hands on her hips.

"EJ! Papi! Let's go!"

Mrs. Santiago is a beautiful puff fish, she has brown cascading hair, a beautiful smile and in her Spanish accent she says... "EJ, vamos." As she turns back to the car, Eggy notices all of the male attention that his mom is getting from the students and even teachers he thinks to himself; "she's loving this." He is alerted to his phone as he receives a text from Ed, "See you tomorrow at school bro." Eggy thinks to himself, *wow, I can't believe they really kicked him out... If I got kicked out, my dad would kill me. And I think my mom would help him hide the body.* Eggy gulps hard erasing that thought from his mind. He remembers his parents saying that morning, that the only reason that he is going to that school is because it's a new project and it looks good for his family. Not to mention, the fact that he's really going to shine. It wasn't that bad being adored all day by teachers and students. He then recalled some cute females that he came in contact with and thought that everything was going to be a breeze. He even had already got one female student to do his homework.

Eggy gets into the car.

His mother looks in her rearview mirror and turns down the loud Spanish music. "Mijo, come te fue en escuela?" (Son, how was your first day of school?) Eggy looks relaxed. "It was smooth. Besides the fact that everyone was trying to get dad's autograph. They already want him to come in and do some motivational speech." Mrs. Santiago laughs, "I'm sure they want a donation. How were those kids there? Were they weird?" "No they were ok but there were some weirdos… but of course, everyone made me look so good." "Of course honey, you're perfect. Your dad wants to know if you went to the athletic department to speak to the coach." Eggy, who realizes that he forgot to do that and doesn't want to upset his mother says, "The coach wasn't around." He had got caught up in his music class, he was amazed by all of the instruments and stayed after class to talk to Mr. Willie who was an even bigger music enthusiast. Mrs. Santiago, seeing her son caught up in a daze breaks him out of it by saying, "Your father just wants you to follow in his footsteps. We're not saying to cut out the music all together but you already have an "in" with baseball…" All of a sudden a song comes on which makes Mrs. Santiago raise the music and begin to dance in her seat as Eggy begins to sway side to side. They both begin to sing along with Elvis Crespo.

"Suavemente, besame, que yo quiero sentir tus labios, besandome otra vez…"

Some of Eggy's favorite memories are the times he spends singing with his mom. With Mrs. Santiago, Eggy never had to hide who he was and what made him happy. She supported him but unfortunately would never go against his dad. Eggy found the same familiar confidant in Mr. Willie today.

Mr. Willie has a large poster of Prince in the music room and Eggy loves Prince's music and how he is adored by all the ladies. Though he asked for Eggy's father's autograph, he took an interest in Mr. Willie when he realized he could discuss his love of music with someone who was just as passionate about it as he was.

Eggy notices how Mrs. Santiago winks at the security guard who opens the gate for her. He loves how, spicy, fiery and independent his mom is. She is the perfect complement to his dad. Mrs. Santiago tames and humbles her husband, or at least tries to. Eggy quietly tries to pass the room where his father is working out without being noticed.

Mr. Santiago is in deep concentration exercising. "1, 2, 3. 4...." Eggy goes into his room and quickly undresses into his underwear. He continues to play the music in his head and starts singing using his brush as a microphone. As he is in mid dance, his mom pokes her head in. "Edgardo, clean up before supper." Eggy continues his dance moves and singing all the way to the bathroom. He looks into the mirror and puffs up as he continues to dance. Eggy gets into the shower, the feel of the water makes him feel free. With soap in hand, he begins to sing a ballad. All of a sudden, everything begins to shake. At first he thought it was just his voice echoing off the marble tiles but then he loses his balance as the soap dropped out of his hand and he falls out of the tub, still singing.

THE AFTERMATH

It's been two days since the ocean shook on the first day of school. The people of Ocean Tides are in hysteria, not knowing what is going to happen next. Stores and schools have been closed but may open next week. While others are out shopping and carrying on their usual weekend routine, the town of Ocean Tides has been glued to their TVs watching the news. (News playing in the background) Reporter: *"The town of Ocean Tides was rocked two days ago with the sudden shaking. Although it caused minimal damage and minor injuries. Officials still don't know what started the shake but will continue to explore it this week."*

Mayor Finnster: *"The citizens of Ocean Tides have nothing to worry about. School will be open again next week. You should all go about your normal routine."* "Damn," Sherman states as he overhears Grandma Turtle's TV while at Marvin's house with Fyn and Marvin. "I was enjoying having no school and doing nothing." Fyn states "What do you think it was? My father thinks it was just something natural that happens and we shouldn't be worried about it." Marvin pops his head out and says, "Something could've hit the ocean and cause more damage than what we thought. Like sometimes space and meteors hit the planets." Sherman looked annoyed, "This isn't one of your books." Grandma Turtle slowly walks into the living room where the boys are and states, "You boys don't know, it's those bubble makers. They're at it again." Fyn and Sherman look at each other and say in unison. "Bubble makers!?"

Marvin pops out again. "You know, the ones that make the bubbles?" Grandma Turtle begins and sits down facing the boys. "You know the strangers of the ocean. You don't want to come in contact with them. Who knows what they're up to?" Sherman asks Fyn if he's ever seen one and Fyn remembers seeing one up close when he and his father went out looking for an exotic seashell when he was a guppy. Grandma Turtle's voice interrupts their conversation. "They're terrible and they will try to take over the ocean." Grandma continues to talk as she walks back to the kitchen. "It's gonna be a war, I tell you. It's gonna be a war."

After Grandma leaves the boys look at each other nervously. Fyn is the first to break the silence, "We *have* to do something."

Jane flips back and forth between Ocean News and O! News. She had just gotten off the phone with her parents who have called every 20 minutes to make sure everything is ok. Since the shake, her parents have spent most of their time at the police station. Jane is angry after hearing the ball outside. Every time the ball bounces, Jane's tentacles begin to spark. She is completely annoyed and turns the TV all the way up. Busy Octo has been outside playing basketball, talking to himself. Busy Octo is uncoordinated with the ball and tends to miss every shot. The ball is thrown into Sherman's front year and Busy Octo goes over to retrieve it. Busy Octo yells "Hey Fyn!" Fyn looks up and passes the ball to Busy Octo. "Hey Mr. Shell and Other Shell." Sherman looks annoyed. "My name is Sherman and this is Marvin." Busy Octo is flustered. "Sorry. Do you guys want to play some basketball?" Marvin excuses himself and runs back into his house. Sherman has to leave and says goodbye to Busy Octo. Fyn walks with Busy Octo to the Jellyfish home. "Did I do something wrong?" Busy Octo looks confused. "You just gotta relax sometimes." Fyn responds.

"What did you think of the shake Busy Octo?"

"I don't know. I shake all the time." As he is walking back into the house he overhears Jane on the phone saying that she wishes that she didn't have a brother. Ashamed, Busy Octo states to himself that he can't do anything right and runs into his room.

Mrs. Prong drops Sherman and Henry in front of The Net located in Ocean Tides. "Are you sure you want to do this Henry? I know your mom said it was your decision." Henry quietly says yes and takes a while before he exits the car. "You'll be here waiting?" Henry looks hopeful. "Yes of course." Mrs. Prong smiles at him reassuringly. "Sherman, you're coming with me right?" Sherman and Henry go up the long staircase. Mrs. Prong yells out the window. "I'll be right here!" Henry and Sherman sit at the glass booth. Well Henry does, Sherman is too small to be seen. Henry is very nervous and as a result keeps picking up and hanging up the phone to make sure it works. Sherman then picks up the phone but clumsily drops it as soon as he sees a huge shark come up from the other side. Mr. Bull Shark's head is as big as the entire glass. His arms don't even fit in his jumpsuit as his muscles are bulging out. Sherman sits quietly next to Henry, not to be seen. Mr. Bull Shark picks up the phone casually. "Henry, you've finally come to see me." Mr. Bull Shark smiles to reveal his huge teeth.

"Hey dad. When are you getting out of here?"

"I don't know. How have you and mom been, you look good. I hope you're staying out of trouble." "Mom had to pick up an extra shift." Henry states looking angry. "And you're not around, why do you care about me being in trouble?!" "I know you're upset Henry, but watch your tone with me." Sherman then pops his head up. "And who's this fella you have with you?" Mr. Bull Shark looks annoyed.

"This is Sherman the shrimp. He's my new friend but you wouldn't know that." "So my son has become a coward. Hanging out with little shrimp. Missing his daddy, probably crying all the time. When will you be a man?" "A man like you? A man who leaves his family. I hope to never be a man like you." Henry slams the phone down and turns away. Sherman jumps on his shoulder to console Henry as they both walk out of The Net together.

"Thanks for being there Sherman."

THE PLAN

As the students are leaving Miss Tutti's class, Fyn is talking to Miss Tutti about the after effects of the shake. "We need to take precautions. We have to be careful. We have to start learning how to be safe." Erica chimes in excitedly. "I can create a PowerPoint presentation on what precautions we need to put in place!" Miss Tutti looks convinced. "I agree; I'll get back to you guys." Miss Tutti makes her way to Miss Marli's office. Miss Marli is eating a sundae and is yelling on the phone to Mr. Omar about where her nuts are. Miss Tutti clears her throat. "Excuse me, Miss Marli, there was no memo but should we discuss with the students about the shake that happened?" Miss Marli talks with her mouth full. "I don't think it's necessary but you're lucky the school didn't shake to the ground or you'd be out of a job."

Eggy is in the music room before class starts. He is on the microphone belting out, "Ocean Tides…...!" Ocean Tides…...!" Mr. Willie smiles, "That sounds really nice Eggy." Eggy looks surprised because he didn't see Mr. Willie enter and says a quiet "*thank you.*"

Fyn comes into the music room and sits in the back with his notebook. He ponders his plan to save the ocean. He's deeply focused until he sees Jane walk into the classroom. Busy Octo is touching everything as usual. Marvin, Sherman and Ed walk in as well. Ed is bragging to Jane that he can play all of the instruments. Sherman turns to Ed, "I don't know how you can play any of them because you're lazy and you have a big fat head." Mr. Willie settles the class down and Henry rushes into the classroom late. "Let's practice the song we did a few days ago with just vocals. On three. One. Two. Three..."

"We're Emotions of the Ocean and we come with love and devotion, for our home of the ocean."

"Cut!" says Willie. "It sounds very (points his finger up and down) …. blah, blah blah…. We need to funk it up. Eggy come here. Give me something." Eggy walks over but looks confused. "I don't know what you mean." "Yes you do. Close your eyes and give me something" Mr. Willie looks at Eggy knowingly. Eggy closes his eyes and belts out…. *"I'M AN EMOOOOOTION!"*

(Busy Octo accidentally hit the table) Mr. Willie looks impressed. "Busy Octo, go on the drums." *"I'm an emotion.* (Drum*) I'm an Emotion of the Ocean. Ocean Tides….!"* The whole class sings after Eggy, "**Ocean Tides**……!"

Ed sings in the background, "**Tides! Tides! Tides! Tides!**"

Jane turns around to face him. "Echo not needed." Marvin gets on the keyboard. Henry hits the table as Busy Octo repeats it on the drums. Edgardo and Jane start to sing, "**Ocean Tides**….!" Henry begins to rap, *"Most of you can't survive in these Ocean Tides. Most of you just get eaten alive. Most of you guys can't survive in the Ocean Tides. They'll eat you alive as you drown in the lies. Looking up for better skies."* Mr. Willie interrupts to say that it sounds very good as everyone begins to congratulate each other. Henry smiles.

Fyn sits in the back of the room listening and it's as if a lightbulb goes off in his head. He blurts aloud, "…Let's have a concert!"

THE SHADOW

"Breaking News! Different types of shadows have been seen around the ocean, specifically in the towns surrounding Ocean Tides. Witnesses have stated that this black shadow tends to follow you and sticks to objects in the ocean. This shadow is to be considered highly dangerous and toxic. It should not come in contact with any ocean creature. It is not yet known if this shadow will pass through or just around Ocean Tides. If you see this shadow, do not attempt to approach it. Hospital officials state that as a result of coming in contact with the shadow, you may experience fever, euphoria, rash, bumps, mutation and loss of limbs or death. They consider this to be highly contagious. We will keep you updated with any new information that we receive. This is Vanessa Mule reporting live for O! News."

Grandma Turtle turns off the TV, then peeks into Marvin's room to make sure he is sleeping. Grandma Turtle begins to think back to the accident which caused the death of Marvin's parents. The Turtles were miners and they suffered a cave in last time the ocean shook, causing many of the miners to get stuck in there. Marvin was just a baby and lost both parents instantly. Grandma Turtle picks up her cane and hobbles back to her bedroom.

***

Miss Tutti is listening to a seminar on TV in which her idol Professor Pierson discusses how teachers should be likeable and have a connection with their students. She goes on to state that students aren't going to learn from anyone they don't like. Miss Tutti is taking notes and is very focused into the seminar as she writes 'teaching is about building relationships." Mr. Willie interrupts her thoughts. "Turn on the news!" As Miss Tutti turns on the news, she and her husband listen to the breaking news of the shadow, mouths agape.

Mr. Finnster is up late making preparations on how to address the concerned citizens of Ocean Tides. The phone rings and Mrs. Finnster hands the phone to her husband stating, "It's Mr. Dolphin." Mr. Finnster takes the call in his office. After speaking with Mr. Dolphin for several minutes, Mrs. Finnster asks her husband what the call was about and he replies slowly…

"The shadow has claimed its first casualty."

Mr. Santiago is speaking to the maintenance guys who are installing his new security system. "So none of that black yucky stuff can come in here right? I have a lot of expensive stuff; I can't have them getting contaminated. By the way, make sure you take off your shoes." He points around the room and speaks in his thick Spanish accent. Mrs. Santiago comes over with her tight spandex outfit on and offers the maintenance man coffee.

All of Ocean Tides head to the community center to hear Mayor Finnster's speech. In the midst of his speech, Fyn and Erica go off together alone so that they can talk. "I overheard my parents talking and I think I know where it started." Erica pulls Fyn and they swim closer to the surface of the water. They soon see seagulls catching their lunch. Fyn is amazed, "I've never been up this far." He looks around curiously. "Just stay close, I'll protect you." Erica says to him. She swims to her right, *"Over here."* She leads Fyn over to a rock and the both of them poke their heads over it.

Up ahead there is a boat and they see puddles of the shadow dripping deeper into the ocean. They also see a boat traveling in the opposite direction from the shadow. There is what they assume to be a bubble maker throwing out a clear liquid behind the boat as he is leaving which seems to clear out the shadows. Not all of the shadow is broken up, several pieces of the shadow fall deeper into the ocean…

Eri and Fyn look at each other in a panic and decide to swim back down. As they swim down, they see some of the shadow following them. Fyn and Erica find themselves racing left, right, up and down to escape it until they feel that the shadows have left them. When they get back to the community center still full of citizens Fyn runs onstage and yells, "Grandma Turtle was right! The bubble makers brought the shadow here. I just saw it for myself." The crowd erupts in an uproar and everyone begins to panic when Fyn suddenly yells;

"The shadow is coming to Ocean Tides! It's coming! It's *coming*! We have to do something!"

His parents convince Fyn to skip school the next day but that doesn't stop him from putting out flyers about the precautions that need to be taken with the shadow. Mrs. Finnster is worried about Fyn when Mr. Finnster attempts to put his wife at ease. "There has been no reported sighting of the shadow in Ocean Tides. You know that Fyn and his friends have a great imagination." Mrs. Finnster agrees but still looks worried. "I know but it's been awhile since I've seen him this worked up… I'm scared honey. I'm scared."

THE SPILL

Miss Marli and Mr. Omar are on their way to the Deep Blue School. "Be careful, Miss Marli; this stuff is moving back here." Mr. Omar tries to keep the steel lid on the bucket in the backseat of the car. "Shut up, Omar, this is such a brilliant idea. They would have to close down the Deep Blue School." Miss Marli's gray eyes light up with excitement. Miss Marli hits a bump, nervously Mr. Omar throws the bucket out of the window after the top falls off. "You idiot!" Miss Marli yells at Mr. Omar. The two rush away from the scene as they see headlights approaching.

Henry is racing home, trying not to miss curfew because his mom will be calling him soon to make sure he is there. As he is riding, he does not notice the shadow until he slips into it and begins to cover him and his bike. Thankfully, his helmet protects his face, not allowing the shadow to get in. Henry remembers feeling suffocated as he awakens in a hospital bed with his mom, Nurse Rebecca at his bedside. Henry's mother looks beautiful but tired. "I guess you really wanted to see me at work Henry," his mom says jokingly, "I'm glad you are ok. I love you so much. Your dad sent these get well flowers too. Your friends are here and if you're up to it, they would like to see you." Before he can answer, his friends rush in - Sherman jumping right on Henry's chest. "I thought we lost you big guy!" Fyn, Marvin, Sherman, Busy Octo, even the Dolphin siblings and Jane come to see Henry. Jane and Erica run up to his bed and kiss him on the cheek. Marvin pokes his head out and winks. Fyn shakes his hand which is wrapped up. Eggy gives him a little radio and states that it's just in case he wants to listen to some music. Ed gives Henry a huge marble, Ed states, "it's supposed to help with positive energy or something like that," he jokes. As everyone gathers around Henry, Fyn states; "We have to do something! This shadow is getting out of the control!" Marvin notices a newspaper and hands it to Fyn to read. Fyn reads, "...the shadow is now in Ocean Tides. It is being suggested that it was possible dumped. Until further notice school will be closed and there will be a curfew - if you don't have to leave your house then do *not*..." Fyn gulps.

A RESTLESS NIGHT

The Emotions of the Ocean have a restless night.

Fyn thinks of what he can do to save Ocean Tides, He further thought about what those bubble makers were pouring to separate the shadow. He called Erica and they spoke on the phone until sun came up, coming up with all sort of ideas to save the school but more so Ocean Tides and even more so, the Ocean. Sherman was curled up in bed reading a note from his step brother. The note was unexpected. His brother wrote that he missed Sherman and stated that everyone had heard about the crisis happening in Ocean Tides. He said that he was worried but asked Sherman to be strong and take care of the family. He further stated that he would be coming there soon… ending the note with, "Love you brother." "*Brother….*" Sherman said to himself and smiled almost shedding a tear.

Jane was in a deep sleep dreaming that she was doing a beauty advertisement selling shampoo/conditioner. Jane was all dressed up and made-up and began running her hands through hair when a sticky black substance comes out and then everything goes dark.

Jane screams herself awake.

Suddenly Ovaltine rushes in her room. "Are you okay Jane!?" Jane answers, "Yes, I must have had a bad dream." "I have been having those too." Ovaline states hesitantly to Jane. Jane replies, "Really…" Ovaltine sits down on her bed before responding, "well I had a dream that the shadow came because of me and that I am not where I belong and it's coming to take me away." Jane looks shocked but then hugs Ovaltine and states, "no matter how much you may annoy me, I love you, and you are the best thing to happen to this family." Jane looks at Ovaline and kisses him on the forehead. "And everything is going to be okay because, you know why?" Ovaltine curiously asks… "*Why?*" Jane smiles down at her little brother. "Because no one messes with *my* brother." Ovaltine smiles back and they hug in a long embrace that lasts several moments.

Fyn, Sherman, Marvin, Ed and Erica are driven to Marvin's house where Mr. and Mrs. Dolphins offered their car service to Eri's friends to go home. Ed stated that he wanted to come for the ride and that he truly wanted to help. They decided to meet at Marvin's house tonight to talk. Eggy couldn't leave his house however, so he had to be informed over the phone. Busy Octo and Jane were already waiting in front of the house for the rest of the gang. You could hear the television blasting from outside and at the same time - Grandma Turtle snoring on the living room couch.

A soon as they walked into Marvin's house and shut the front door they see papers and boxes everywhere half opened filled with protection gear, masks, gloves etc. The Ocean Shopping Network is also on selling body suits for protection. Marvin cuts off the television and at that very moment, Grandma Turtle is awoken and sits up in a fighting stance with her cane. "It's just us Grandma."

Grandma Turtle smiles and relaxes "...well aren't you little one's trouble, sneaking up on old Grandma like that." She places her cane down and looks over the bunch with warm eyes. Fyn smiles before asking what all the stuff in the living room was. Grandma Turtle answers cooly, "You never can be too ready or prepared." Marvin is annoyed and tells his Grandma "You are always going overboard with everything... Do you know what they say about you? That say you are crazy!" Grandma Turtle retorts, "I don't care what no one thinks about me. I know who I am and who I aint!" She stands up firmly and straightens out her dress before sitting back down. "You see little ones..." she motions for the gang to come closer and they all gather around her, sitting down and intensely listening to Grandma Turtle. Marvin is even more annoyed, his shell feeling tight around his little frame... but his ears are open for another one of his grandma's crazy stories. Grandma Turtle starts in a quiet tone "What the news aint tell you is that this happened *years* ago. I am talking about a long time back when, even before any of your parents were born. The Bubble Makers were up to something and there was a terrible explosion and there was fire everywhere. The water was hot and there were areas you couldn't go. There was smoke so thick that you couldn't see and that sticky black substance was everywhere. Though the Bubble Makers tried to clear it, it just went deeper into the ocean affecting our community. There were many fatalities and several injuries. If you did survive, you have some type of reminder of that time. We call that time the Dark Waves. I remember that time every day..." Grandma Turtle becomes silent and she slowly lifts up her robe to reveal that her left leg is just a nub. She is missing the lower half of her leg, it stopped at her knee. Marvin runs to his Grandma and cries, holding her. "I didn't know! I didn't *know*!" All of theEmotions of the Ocean children look tearful as they look at Grandma in admiration. Grandma looks at them, "You know everyone serves a purpose in your life. You guys are friends because you bring out the best in each other. You lift each other up. It's good to be surrounded by people like that. They bring out the best in you. Let me get some rest, I think I've had enough excitement for one day. Good night little ones."

TheEmotions of the Ocean decided to call it a night and go home to get some rest. Though thoughts of dark waves swam in their dreams.

***

Erica stands in front of the classroom with Miss Tutti while she attempts to get the children's attention in one of the auditoriums of the Ocean Tides Community Center. Both the Deep Blue School and the Ocean Tides Public Schools have been closed due to sightings of the shadow. Fights have already broken out in addition to name calling amongst the children. This has been going on since the bell rang signaling the beginning of the period almost 10 minutes ago.

Erica speaks up. "We all have to find a way to get along, so we can come up with a solution." Miss Tutti then states, "To assist with homework, we are going to pair up children from both schools. So please listen carefully as your buddy assignments are stated. Sheila and Marvin. Ronald and Sherman. Ovaltine and Tatiana." This goes on through the period until all of the children are matched up with partners. Fyn runs excitedly to the front of the classroom. "Hey everyone, Erica and I came up with an idea to help save Ocean Tides! We need to raise awareness around the Ocean about what is going on here before this situation gets bigger." The kids make kissing noises and throw seaweed at Fyn to heckle him.

Mr. Finnster is on the evening news addressing the citizens of Ocean

Tides. "As a way to raise funds to assist in the cleanup of Ocean Tides during this terrible tragedy and to build a dome to ensure that this does not happen again. Edgardo Santiago Sr. has graciously offered to organize a charity baseball game with his former team, the Waveville Tigers against their former nemesis Marine Blue Lions. Geoffrey, the former captain of the Marine Blue Lions appears over Mr. Finnster's shoulder via satellite. "I can't wait to face off with Edgardo again. I've been waiting since they stole the champion from us 10 years ago to have the opportunity to show them how much they stink. I'm happy to come play." The game is announced for two weeks from today. The funds are being raised and Ocean Tides is being prepped for cleanup. Mr. Finnster is excited because of the celebrity presence and the money raised with help Ocean Tides. "This is going to bring a lot of money to Ocean Tides. I don't want anything to ever happen to my city again. Our children live here, we fell in love here, I love this city. If this event and this little 'drama' is going to bring attention to Ocean Tides, then let's play ball." Even though all anyone can talk about is the upcoming charity baseball game, what Eggy looks forward to most of all is his music classes with Mr. Willie.

"*Do, re, me, fa, so, la, ti….*" Eggy sings as Mr. Willie plays the piano. Children from both schools are already formed in groups. Fyn asks Sherman what is wrong as he senses Sherman's distance. "Henry isn't doing well and they won't let me see him." Sherman answers, looking disappointed. Ed overhears him and chimes in, "Then we're just gonna need to sneak in there and find out what's up." Fyn interrupts. "You know I had a dream that we did a concert and raised money. Wouldn't that be cool?" Jane rushes to Fyn's side and smiles. "How did I look?" Marvin hears her and retorts with a loud, "Beautiful!" from inside his shell and everyone laughs. Mr. Willie stops playing, "A concert. Now that would be a good idea." Ronald, a tiger shark from the public school disagrees. "A concert with these freaks?! I don't think so!" The other public school kids laugh. Before anyone else can respond, the bell rings.

There is big excitement throughout the ocean about Ocean Tides. People cannot stop talking about the charity baseball game and even more, raising funds for the common disaster that happened in the ocean. Middle schoolers Fyn and Erica have been on television several times raising awareness about the cause during different segments of the news, discussing the benefits that the dome will bring to Ocean Tides.

On the days leading up to the game, there is a high anticipation throughout the ocean. Those who cannot attend the game plan to be glued to their TVs ready with the telephone number to make a donation. Edgardo Sr. is in the batting cage in the basement practicing the night before the game when his son Eggy enters. "Mom said you wanted to see me." Edgardo Sr. stops and turns to face his son. "Yes, mom said you wanted to sing the national anthem. Now don't get me wrong, I think it's cool that you're in this singing thing but I was thinking more like you could throw the first pitch." "Dad why would I want to throw out the first pitch. This is about you, not about me." "No, this isn't about me. This is about our family and how we're saving the town. Everyone is going to love me. And love you and love our family. We're saving the town."

Eggy walks away as he hears his father muttering.

"It's gonna be great Eggy…" his dad continued. "I'm gonna get another chance. It's gonna be great Eggy, *it's gonna be great.*"

TO SAVE THE OCEAN

An hour and a few towns away, the Marine Blue Lions bus is traveling Coral Reef Way heading towards Ocean Tides. They are singing on the bus "Cage those tigers, lock the door! We're the lions, hear us roar!" The ride became a little bumpy, as the water became a little foggy and smoky. As the ocean became murky, the tires slipped on a black substance that soon began to cover the bus.

The players on board hurried to lock the windows so that the substance couldn't enter the bus while the driver called for help. While calling, the driver realized that the sticky substance would not allow the bus to move before abruptly getting disconnected and hearing nothing but white noise…

The players huddled together as the shadow relentlessly stuck to their bus, unable to come inside. Mr. Finnster paces nervously after hearing from the Coral Reef Way Patrol that the Marine Blue Lions were in a bad spill and it was taking hours to get them out. The entire team was hours away and they would not arrive in time to play. Overhearing his father on the phone, Fyn rushes out of the house. Ocean Tides Memorial Stadium is already filling up and the Waveville Tigers are already on the field practicing with Edgardo Sr. signing autographs. Fyn frantically runs around town leaving messages for his friends to meet him at Mr. Willie's room in one hour. He states that it's an emergency and Mr. Willie needs their help. All of theEmotions of the Ocean children show up in Mr. Willie's classroom – that's Marvin, Sherman, Busy Octo, Ed, Eri, Jane and Eggy. They all look confused when they don't see Mr. Willie but ask Fyn what is going on. "I overheard my dad on the phone, the Marine Blue Lions bus ran into the shadow! They are not going to make it in time. I think we should perform a concert!" Mr. Willie who saw the children rushing towards his classroom, enters with Miss Tutti. "What are you kids doing in here? Why aren't you getting ready to watch the game?" Miss Tutti looks equally concerned and asks, "Is everything okay Fyn?" Fyn explains to Miss Tutti and Mr. Willie about what he overheard and of the concert. Erica, Ed and Jane are excited about the idea. Busy Octo and Sherman are doubtful. Marvin, is of course, fearful.

Sherman looks at Fyn and makes a face. "Everyone is coming here to see two famous baseball teams. Nobody is gonna want to see us." He thinks of his brothers who just came into town and who will be in the stands today. "I don't know Fyn; there are some songs we haven't even finished let alone rehearsed." Mr. Willie says. Eggy chimes in. "I can lead. I think we can do this." To everyone's surprise, Marvin pokes his head out of his shell. "I think we CAN do this…. *together.*" TheEmotions of the Ocean gather their instruments and head towards the stadium grounds.

***

When they enter the stadium again, Mayor Finnster is making the announcement that the Marine Blue Lions bus has had an incident. As a result, the game is cancelled. Mr. Edgardo is insistent that the game can proceed against the Waveville Tigers… he motions for fans to come down to the field and for some to even join the game. He's obsessed with continuing the game and doesn't want his fans to miss an opportunity to see him play despite the fact that his own team members are packing up to leave. The fans are confused and upset after making donations that there will be no game to attend.

TheEmotions of the Ocean approach the field with their instruments alongside Mr. Willie and Miss Tutti. Mr. Willie comes out with an electric guitar and plays the beginning verse of 'When Doves Cry' by Prince. Busy Octo plays the drums as Eggy takes over the vocals and Fyn takes over the guitar, moving his mohawk back and forth with the beat. Jane and Ed perform backup vocals as Sherman grabs a tambourine and Marvin mans the keyboards. Eggy gets very into singing and begins dancing, almost as if he's singing directly to his father. Eggy starts dancing across the stage.

The people that have gathered on the field take their seats and look at the children with amusement, clearly enjoying the show.

Grandma Turtle watches the scene unfold on TV and mutters to herself, "these kids are out of their minds" as she calls to make a donation. Henry watches from his hospital bed and quickly gets up to go join his friends.

The crowd applauds for the children who form a single file so they are all on the same level. They sing along together in a slow catchy melody as Marvin steps up playing the keyboard and nervously pokes his head out of his shell. Together they sing, "We areEmotions of the Ocean, and we give our love and devotion, to our home of the ocean." Individually they sing loudly;

"I'M AN EMOTION! I'M AN EMOTION!"

Fyn is the last to sing as he says alone, "We're all emotions! We're *all emotions!*" The crowd gets quiet as they anticipate the children's next move. Eggy steps up and sing. "Ocean Tides......."

Jane joins him in the song. "Baby......"

The rest of the children join in. "Ocean Tides......"

Unexpectedly and out of nowhere, Henry runs on stage with a microphone. Henry raps, "I'm anEmotions of the Ocean, and Ocean Tides is where I reside. And these tides could bury you alive. So you gotta stay strong and try to survive." Henry surprisingly sees his father in the crowd surrounded by security smiling at him chanting, "Go Henry!" He smiles confidently and continues, *"We all make mistakes but we are all in this together. With our fins we could win. Let's do this together. Say what, what! Donate, yeah I'm talking to you. Clean up Ocean Tides, so we can have anew. Donate yeah I'm talking to you, clean up Ocean Tides so we can have anew!"* There is a standing ovation for the children at the end of the song. Mayor Finnster rushes to inform the crowd that the city has received enough funds from donations from all over the ocean. TheEmotions of the Oceans' families come up to the stage to give their children hugs. The Prong family come on stage, the brothers wearing army fatigue hug Sherman and tell him how proud they are of him.

The Jellyfish family is there to embrace Busy Octo and Jane. They feel like a complete family now as Jane gives Busy Octo a kiss on the forehead. Mr. and Mrs. Dolphin come to congratulatc Ed and Erica. Erica runs over to Fyn and gives him a kiss as he turns completely red.

"We did it Fyn!" Sheila the clam goes on stage to find Marvin, tells him what a great job he did and gives him a kiss on his shell. Even Edgardo Santiago Sr. comes to the stage, feeling embarrassed of himself but overall proud that theEmotions of the Oceans pulled off such a feat and hugs his son. "Great job son."

Fyn winks at Miss Tutti and gives her a microphone. Miss Tutti and Mr. Willie begin to sing Whitney Houston's "Greatest Love of All" as all the families begin to depart the stage. Rebecca Bull Shark gives her son, Henry, a hug – who swam all the way there to be with them and says, "You know you shouldn't be out in your condition." Henry smiles. "I feel great mom. I've never felt better." Henry searches the crowd, "You see dad?" Rebecca looks up into the stands where her husband was watching her and they see the police officers scattered everywhere. There is an empty chair with handcuffs dangling from it. They hear the officers on their walkie talkies, "Henry Bull Shark Sr. has escaped! I repeat, Henry Bull Shark Sr. has escaped!"

WE DID IT

"Now as you can guess, those children raised enough money to save Ocean Tides" Mr. Blue says in the mirror as he ties his tie. "The Marine Blue Lions came to somewhat of a truce with the Waveville Tigers by making a hefty donation to help clean Ocean Tides." In his own words, the captain stated, "Edgardo Santiago Jr. has a beautiful voice but his father's team still stinks!" Mr. Blue smiles amused. "A rematch is planned for some time in the future." "Ocean Tides has been rebuilt with steel walls designed for protection. Fyn and Erica have been traveling all over the ocean as part of an internship, educating others on the dangers of the shadow."

Mr. Blue admires his self before turning around to continue.
As far as the rest of theEmotions of the Ocean......"

"Ed has decided that he wants to be a surgeon like his father and has been interning at the hospital and flirting with the nurses."

"Marvin has been spending some time out of his shell with Sheila and continues to be entertained by Grandma Turtle's antics as she continues to care for the children of the neighborhood."

"Sherman used all his anger and energy to join the track team and become one of the fast runners in Ocean Tides. Henry is there at every meet to show his support."

"Henry has gone to many different schools to talk about bullying and to discuss how having a parent in The Net can have an impact on a child. At times, he still thinks he sees his father who has not been found and is still wanted."

"Busy Octo plays on the drumline and is very popular and Jane is a cheerleader, no one talks about her brother."

Mr. Blue pauses to put on his dark blue blazer.

"I guess you're wondering what happened with Miss Marli and Mr. Omar. They were caught on camera by the Jellyfish detectives after Omar broke down and told the whole story about how they released the shadow into Ocean Tides. Now they do clean up at the local junkyard as part of their community service."

"And as far as the Deep Blue School, Miss Tutti became principal and often students from the Public School come down to offer their tutoring services. They have built a great relationship. When Mr. Willie is not teaching his music class, he is playing music at a local cafe with Edgardo and Busy Octo on the weekends."

"And as for me…" Mr. Blue picks up a rose and gives himself one final look in the mirror and smiles. "I have the pleasure of sharing the company of the *lovely* Blanche Turtle tonight."

The End.

STAY TUNED FOR OTHER BOOKS IN THE Emotions of the Ocean SERIES

About The Author

Creator and author of the Emotion of the Ocean series, Tania Isley-Robinson has a bachelor's degree in psychology and has 20 years of experience in the mental health field. Tania has worked with a diverse population and has a great passion for helping people. Tania also has personal experience in the mental health field, being diagnosed with Bipolar Disorder.

Tania's love for marine life plus her childlike imagination has aided her in creating characters who are warm, funny, and relatable which makes it easy to fall in love with them.

Tania states that these characters are a representation of some of the children that she has worked with in her career. Tania looks forward to sharing more stories from her series and hopes that these characters will come alive in order to assist children in expressing themselves; as well as educating our youth and their families on mental health and the importance of self-care.

Follow the author and the Emotions of the Ocean series at
www.BlackGoldPublishing.com

Made in the USA
Middletown, DE
15 January 2023

22207801R00035